Creepy Things Are Scaring Me

by Jerome and Jarrett Pumphrey
illustrated by Rosanne Litzinger

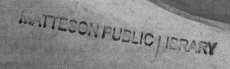

HarperCollins*Publishers*

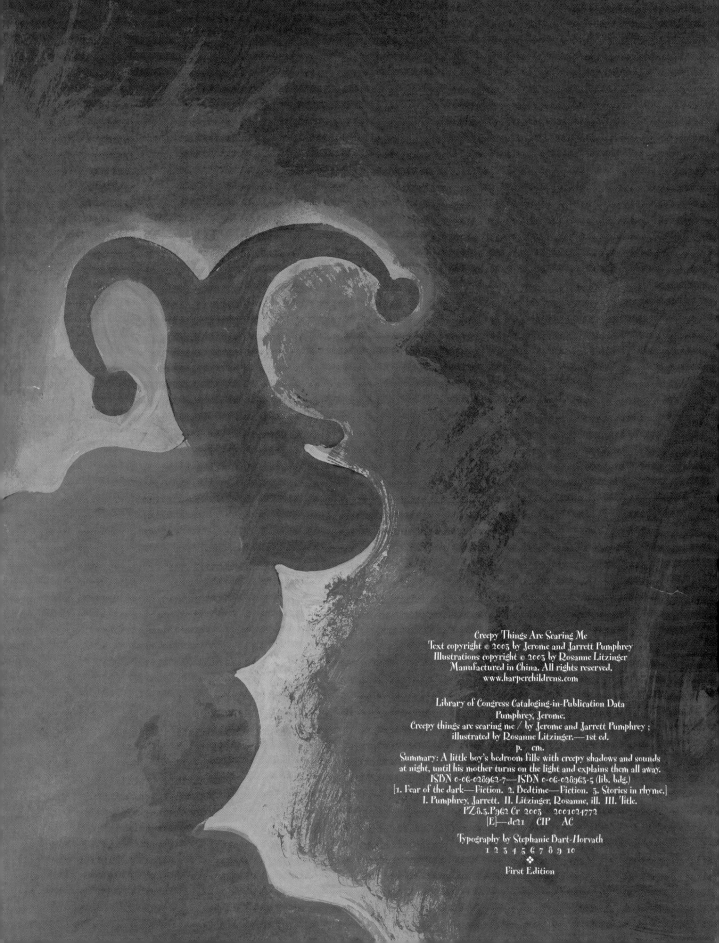

Creepy Things Are Scaring Me
Text copyright © 2003 by Jerome and Jarrett Pumphrey
Illustrations copyright © 2003 by Rosanne Litzinger
Manufactured in China. All rights reserved.
www.harperchildrens.com

Library of Congress Cataloging-in-Publication Data
Pumphrey, Jerome.
Creepy things are scaring me / by Jerome and Jarrett Pumphrey ;
illustrated by Rosanne Litzinger.—1st ed.
p.   cm.
Summary: A little boy's bedroom fills with creepy shadows and sounds
at night, until his mother turns on the light and explains them all away.
ISBN 0-06-028962-7—ISBN 0-06-028963-5 (lib. bdg.)
[1. Fear of the dark—Fiction. 2. Bedtime—Fiction. 3. Stories in rhyme.]
I. Pumphrey, Jarrett. II. Litzinger, Rosanne, ill. III. Title.
PZ8.3.P962 Cr 2003   2001024772
[E]—dc21   CIP   AC

Typography by Stephanie Bart-Horvath
1 2 3 4 5 6 7 8 9 10
❖
First Edition

To moms and dads who leave the hall light
on—especially ours, who always did
—J.P. and J.P.

To all scaredy-cats
—R.L.

Mama kisses me good-night.

Mama then turns out the light.

The room gets dark.
The room gets creepy.

The room's *soooooo* dark that I'm not sleepy.

A creepy sound beneath my bed!

I want to run. . . .

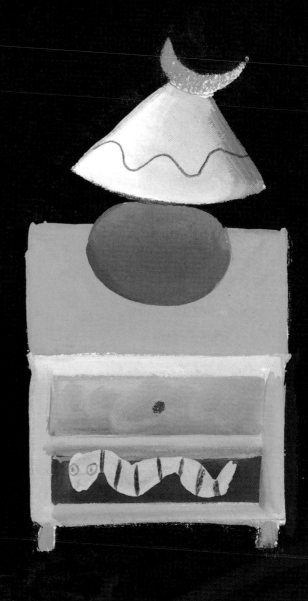

I'll hide instead.

A creepy thing is on the ceiling. . . .

It gives me such a creepy feeling.

A creepy monster on the wall. . . .

I would feel safer in the hall!

A creepy shadow on the floor. . . .

I can't hide here anymore!

Mama! Mama! Come and see!

Creepy things are scaring me!

A creepy shadow's on the floor!

It's just the tree and nothing more.

Well, there's something creepy on the ceiling!

It's just cold air that you are feeling.

And the creepy monster on the wall?!

It's just your teddy bear. That's all.

But I heard a sound beneath my bed!

It's just your puppy. There's his head.

Now the room is not so creepy.
Now I'm feeling kind of sleepy.

Mama then turns out the light.

Mama kisses me good-night.